Story

Kingdom

Develop your child's thinking skills and build emotional resilience

Stories sit at the heart of what it means to be human. We tell stories all the time. We make sense of the world and our place in it through the stories we tell and the stories we hear. This is true across all cultures. Each has its own wealth of story tradition and story is a universal human achievement and an elegant means of celebrating the cultural diversity which invigorates and enriches our society.

Young children are particularly receptive to the rich world of metaphor present in good stories. They don't get bogged down in trying to "figure out" the story, but enter into it with the full power of their imaginations. It is natural for all of us, particularly the young child, to describe and understand objects, events and ideas in terms of how they are "like" other objects, events and ideas. Consider for a moment the colourful world inhabited by the kindergarten or reception age child. Observe how the "dressing-up" box becomes a doorway into a different universe, a metaphorical realm where they can "act as if" they are the teacher or the parent or a character from one of the multitude of stories they have already heard or seen. One need only picture the familiar sight of a miniature Elsa enthusiastically 'letting it go' to recognise the power of imagination in the child's life. These are the foundations of the rich metaphorical world inhabited by the child, a world which, if nurtured, grows and evolves with them to refine their perceptions and equip them with ever more sophisticated patterns from which to respond to the world.

A wealth of research now suggests that data; the facts and figures, is no longer absolute monarch. Of course, it is possible to use facts and figures to inform and deliver information, but the evidence suggests that story and narrative are a more effective way to engage and convince, to motivate and promote meaning and empathy. Our brains, it appears, are hard-wired neurologically to respond to stories, particularly character driven stories.

Ironically, and tragically, the world of Education seems to be careering headlong in the opposite direction, with an ever-increasing obsession with measurement and the collection and proliferation of data.

Storytelling has long been a source of delight and entertainment, but it is vastly more than that. Metaphor is the language of the brain. Stories provide patterns and templates through which we make sense of our world and our place in it. Of course, we need the data; the facts, the numbers....and we need to manage that data. But the data is not the story, it exists to help us tell the story. The approach proposed in these pages understands the power of story and integrates it into the learning process. We live in an age where there are more platforms from which to tell our stories than ever before in human history, along with a plethora of stories competing for our children's attention. It is of vital importance that the stories we tell our children are carefully selected to nurture and nourish them as thinkers, learners and emotionally resilient, happy people.

It is possible for an adult to place themselves between the young child's spontaneous response to each new experience of the world in order to shape and guide that experience. The adult can invest the encounter with purpose, focus attention on what is important and help the child to interpret the meaning of events. Connections can be made with prior learning in the child's life, highlighting how things are related to one another. Anyone who has tried to change the rules of a game, or alter details of a familiar story and has experienced the outrage this provokes in young children, will be acutely aware of their need for order and predictability. When a child is helped to connect prior learning and experience to what is happening now, it supports that child in experiencing the world as a more ordered, secure place. This sense of safety and order is, in my view, a pre-requisite for all subsequent learning. The child who has experienced this sense of order and safety is better prepared to generate such order in their own emotional life in the midst of an increasingly complex and potentially confusing world. In this way the child is helped to weave an ever-richer tapestry of knowledge about the world and their place and potential within it. Stories are the perfect vehicle for achieving this in a way that is joyful and enriching for both adult and child. It is a natural process which complements and extends the child's direct and spontaneous response to the world around them.

If we can better understand the exchange of attention which occurs when a story is told, we can create an opportunity to go beyond the use of story as merely an enjoyable time filler or entertainment and utilize its power to enrich the metaphorical patterns through which children give meaning to their experience. I would like to take a look at how we can shape the quality of our interactions with children in order to harness some of the potential of their natural open-ness to metaphor.

For millennia knowledge has been passed on via story, transmitting cultural values, and even the very building blocks of thinking, from one generation to the next. Story-telling, if approached with skill and understanding, can provide opportunities for children to compare and classify, leading to greater skill and discernment in decision making. By listening to stories unfold in sequence, a child learns to restrain impulsive responses in favour of more considered ones. Skills in interpreting and predicting are developed. Through story we can nurture an internal need for comprehension and the search for meaning. Planning behaviour (i.e. gathering information, identifying resources, noting potential obstacles, developing strategies etc) can be promoted in the search for solutions to the dilemmas presented in stories. In a very natural way, children can be encouraged to move beyond the immediate world of concrete objects to begin to think conceptually.

So far, we have focused on thinking and cognition, but the child, indeed the human, exists in an emotional world as well as a cognitive one. The boundary between the kingdoms of thinking and emotion is an indistinct and malleable one. A child's emotions can be immensely powerful and we do them a dis-service if we fail to provide them with the thinking tools necessary for managing the very strong emotions which might otherwise overwhelm them. Story, skilfully used, offers a safe world in which to develop the skills to tame and manage the 'wild beasts' of emotion. 'Thinking' and 'emotion' are not opposing forces, both systems have evolved to work together for the benefit of the individual and, it could be argued, for society. What appear as spontaneous, emotional, intuitive reactions are often a consequence of past behaviour in response to emotional arousal, processed, and evaluated by the 'thinking' brain. How successful was our response? Did it keep us safe? Did it create more problems? Viewed through this lens, emotion is, clearly, a key component of our humanity and even of our thinking. This requires a caveat. While emotions, rightly guided, can be true and loyal servants, if the child is not assisted in developing the thinking skills required to harness and channel emotions, the same emotions can easily become cruel and tyrannical masters. In the world of Story, the child is empowered to explore the nature of relationships, develop empathy, identify threat. In story the child experiences the safety of being psychologically removed from the events, an observer who can step back into the safety of parental arms or the classroom story corner whenever they choose. In the story, a child can be exposed to disappointments, frustrations and dangers in a way which serves as a form of inoculation, affording a degree of protection on their road to developing as individuals. Similarly, the child experiences joy and sadness, injustice and reward within the same tale. A child exposed to a wealth of rich and varied stories will be equipped to face the inevitable challenges of life, knowing that there is also great beauty in the world.

There are three key principles to keep in mind if we wish to harness the power of story to support the cognitive and emotional development of our children:

1. **Be aware of what you want to achieve.** If storytelling is a natural process, why write a book about it? The power of a story is greatly

enhanced when it is done with intention. The experience is enriched when the story-teller knows and communicates the intended outcome of the interaction/ learning experience, engaging and responding to the listener. (e.g. "This is a story about what happens when ……")

Even the "once upon a time" formula can provoke a profound, almost magical state of focussed attention in children. This is a natural learning state. The child has been alerted as to what they might be looking out for. Even if a person is 'looking for a needle in a hay stack', it helps if they know it's a needle they are looking for! While the adult should have an awareness of their intention when approaching a story, this should not be rigid or over-prescriptive. The child/ children may well bring thoughts and observations of their own, and this is to be encouraged.

2. **What does it mean?** The "why" of the interaction; what is the purpose, how will it help, what does it mean? ("Why was Jack's mum angry when he sold the cow for five magic beans?" "How do we know she was angry?" "If she is angry with Jack, does this mean she doesn't love him anymore?")

3. **Finding the analogy**- The exploration of how the situation is "like" other objects, events and ideas beyond the current context. Principles which arise in the story can be "bridged" to other areas of the child's experience helping to generalize learning. e.g. The above example from Jack and the Beanstalk could lead to a broader discussion about times when a child has experienced anger, their own or that of others. What happened? How did it feel? Did things turn out ok in the end? What helped? Is there anything that could be done differently next time? Is anger always bad?

Stories and thinking:

So, what is thinking? Thinking begins with a question, a need, a problem. many stories present us with a dilemma; a problem to be solved. This can be the springboard for all sorts of thinking:

- **Symbolic thinking** –A symbol is something which represents or means something else.
- **Sequencing** – Considering the order in which events occur.
- **Problem solving** – Identifying the nature of the "problem" and developing strategies for reaching a solution.
- **Inferential thinking** – "Reading between the lines"

- **Imagining** – The capacity to consider and think about things which are not immediately present in time or space. In order to do this, we must utilize the peculiarly human capacity for complex, abstract language with past, present and future tenses.
- **Flexibility** - Considering a different way of approaching the problem/ situation
- **Evaluation/ critical thinking** – Looking for logical evidence before making decisions. Also considering the quality of decisions and/ or actions within a story. (even quite young children can develop their capacity for such thinking if it is

presented in a way they can connect with).

Anyone who has spent any time telling stories to young children knows that the story inevitably leads to new questions and new problems to be solved. This is good news! When a child has new problems to solve it means that they are being extended and challenged – this is essential for healthy development on both an emotional and a cognitive level. The stories contained in this collection may, on first reading, appear to be presented in language which is of a fairly high level. Some might say too high for the intended audience. There are two key responses to this, one is addressed below; the stories do not have to be read out verbatim. They can be read by the adult, with the basic pattern and structure absorbed. The adult can then tell the story with the language level adapted as required. However, one must also consider that when a baby is born, we do not wait until they grow up before speaking to them. Children's capacity for the acquisition of language is extraordinary and we do them a disservice if we are overly insistent on 'dumbing-down' the language we use when talking to them. The great Russian psychologist Lev Vygotsky offered us the concept of the 'Zone of Proximal Development'. This suggests that learning should be pitched at the level between what the child can achieve unaided and that which they are able to achieve with support. The language we use with children should draw then forward into the next, or proximal, level of development.

Telling the Story: Practical Tips

- Reading stories is, of course, great. A joyful association with books is a powerful aid in the development of literacy, but I also suggest you try telling stories too rather than always reading them. Trust yourself. This is not to say you should try to "memorize" the story, just note in your mind various "signposts" or important points in the story and work creatively from one point to the next. This is a skill which develops quickly with a little practice.

- While the adult should approach the story with intention regarding the thinking skills to be highlighted and the potential for enhancing wellbeing, the focus should remain on telling the story. Try to avoid over-interpreting the story or analysing the magic out of it. Meanings can be elicited from younger children, but "ask, don't tell" should be the guiding principle.

- The effective telling of a story doesn't require an "over the top" performance. Good eye-contact with the listener(s) and subtle changes of tone will hold attention just as well as big gestures and volume and can often be more conducive to learning.

- Don't be afraid to create your own stories. This works particularly well with young children: Create a character with whom the child can identify, present a simple dilemma, obstacle or problem facing the character and then bring in some "helpers" to assist our character towards a resolution. This simple formula is always a winner!

- Remember, empower yourself as a storyteller! Trust yourself to tell the story rather than read it. This not only makes for a more engaging story, but also enables you to establish a much better quality of connection with the listener. The pay-off for you as the teller of the story is that it raises your sense of status, autonomy and achievement.

Metaphors and the Brain

There has been much interest in recent years as to the different functions of the right and left hemispheres of the brain. Much of the research supports the educational value of story and metaphor. The Left brain, we are told, is linear, sequential and analytic. The right brain, however, recognizes patterns in an "all at once", immediate way. The right brain takes in spatial relationships, sensory information and a range of very subtle stimuli which the left brain doesn't perceive.

It may be the case that good stories provide information which connects with the left and right brain simultaneously. In our everyday lives the left brain is generally 'in charge', but if it's dealing with "its own stuff", the right brain is freed to receive the other, perhaps more subtle messages. This implies an opportunity to go beyond mere acquisition of information to understand the world at a deeper level. One might call this the development of wisdom. Stories offer us a powerful way of sneaking past the "guards at the gates of the castle". The ability to learn in a spontaneous way from the metaphors held in stories taps into a natural learning state and is fundamental to finding meaning in our lives.

....and they all lived happily ever after!?

Imagination is a powerful cognitive tool. It enables us to bring the past back to life, reflect, evaluate what worked and what didn't, plan strategies for how things could be done better, even generate new realities. A child can, however, "mis-imagine". They can create erroneous or unhelpful "stories" about themselves and who they are. Amidst the noise of the myriad distractions available to a child today, the all-pervading media, accessed through countless devices, presents a barrage of stories, not all of them helpful. The beautiful simplicity of a carefully selected story, rich with positive suggestions and patterns, delivered with the gift of your full attention (a gift of incalculable value) can help restore the balance.

A pivotal moment in this realisation of how fundamental story is to being human occurred, for me, many years ago when my daughter was around 2 1/2 years old. She loved stories. Every day was filled with stories; stories from books, stories acted out with her toys, even stories watched on video (for one summer, she had a particular fascination with Disney's Snow

White, which she insisted upon watching pretty much every day…..I can still recite most of the movie verbatim!) One evening as I settled her down to sleep, she asked, as usual, for a story. Things had been busy at work and I was tired. I wearily reached for one of the many story-books on the shelf, only to be met by a very vocal protest and much furious shaking of her little head. I had clearly made some sort of fairly serious error! 'No, no, no!' she said. 'I don't want a story from a book, I want a story from….from…from your tummy!'

What she meant, of course, was that she wanted me to tell her a story, as I often did, making it up as I went, rather than read one from a book. Apart from melting my heart and being unbelievably cute, this taught me something of the power of stories, told directly, with connection and eye contact and the wonderful, powerful exchange of attention which takes place. To my daughter it was, quite literally, visceral. These stories came from inside me, from my 'tummy'.

Even now, all these years later, I glow inside when I think of that moment.

I hope the stories presented here offer a starting point; a springboard into the vast potential of story and metaphor as a tool for the cognitive and emotional development of the children in our care. The stories you tell a child can be gifts which serve them for a lifetime and time spent telling stories is precious time.

Using this book in a school setting:

Children are not immune to the ever-increasing complexity and stress of life. Our children's senses are bombarded with information all day every day. In no time at all that information is redundant, replaced with a new set of systems, concepts and vocabulary.

It is no longer enough simply to teach our children lists of instructions for approaching life and learning which worked in the past. We must provide them with a map of the terrain which enables them to avoid the inevitable swamps and pitfalls and navigate their own way through the learning journey and, indeed, their life journey.

The complex and often brutal world of social media, which is so central to the way our children now live their lives, brings a whole new set of challenges. It is little wonder that an ever-increasing number of children experience levels of anxiety and emotional arousal so high that effective learning becomes near impossible. This collection of stories, and the approach to using them suggested in this book exists to give children the necessary thinking tools to negotiate the complex and challenging social and learning environment in which they exist and to regain control of their emotional world.

The world of Education is waking up to the impact of adverse childhood experiences on learning. Why has this taken so long? It seems self-evident that a child, exposed to trauma in any of its dark forms, will view the world as inherently unstable, inherently dangerous and threatening. Surely one does not even need the evidence of recent research to understand that such experiences would lock themselves deep in the psyche of a child and influence their subsequent responses in the world. It stands to reason.

What is becoming increasingly evident from the research, however, is just how deep the impact goes; dramatically reducing not only life chances, but also health outcomes and even actual life expectancy.

The research does not leave us without cause for hope. With the right kinds of intervention, the minds of children can be extraordinarily resilient. This mental resilience does appear to lead to healing physically, emotionally, and dare I say, spiritually. It is my heartfelt belief that story has a profound and useful part to play. I believe it to be one of those 'right kinds of intervention' Recent years have seen an apparent increase in awareness of the impact of adverse childhood experiences and the 'trauma-informed' classroom is an encouraging development which is gaining ground in educational settings internationally. The Scottish Government has recognised this looming crisis and has pledged £60,000,000 for the development of Counselling services in schools. This is a welcome and necessary initiative which is to be applauded, but I believe it is only part of the answer. To improve the mental and emotional wellbeing of our children we must, I believe, take a two-pronged approach. Children who are experiencing mental health challenges must, of course, receive support which clearly identifies and responds to their needs, but to promote good mental health and wellbeing in all children, we must provide a secure grounding in the thinking tools and practical self-care knowledge and strategies they will need to manage and thrive in the increasingly complex world in which they live. With this in mind, this book and the 'Story Kingdom' approach suggested are of equal value to the parent offering a bedtime story to their own child as to the primary school teacher or, indeed, the secondary school nurture group teacher providing those essential life skills to those in their care. More than this, they offer to empower children to protect the boundaries of their own Kingdom.

While this book and the stories contained in it can be used 'straight out of the box', their power and impact in the lives of children will be greatly enhanced if they are used regularly as the core of a Thinking Skills and Emotional Wellbeing 'syllabus'. Training packages are available for parents, schools and other organisations wishing to get the most out of the transformative potential of this approach.

The 'Story Kingdom' Method:

The transformative power of stories can be accessed effectively by employing a simple structure I refer to as 'The Story Kingdom' method. This presents a metaphor for the child's internal 'kingdom' of thought and emotion and provides a structure for organising and managing that world.

1. **The King's (Queen's/ Sovereign's) advisors.** For the sake of convenience and brevity I use the term 'King' here, but this can, of course, be substituted with Queen, or Sovereign, or King/ Queen together as appropriate. The 'King' represents the executive faculties of a child's thinking. The 'King' makes the decisions after considering the evidence presented to him by his 'advisors'. The 'advisors' represent different aspects of the child's

emotional and thought life and potential areas for discussion will fall into one of these categories. There are three 'advisors':

- **The 'Bard'.** The 'Bard' is a musician and poet and represents that part of the child's interior world concerned with emotional connection, empathy and creativity. Without the balance provided by the 'Guardian' and the 'Court Scientist', this aspect of the interior Kingdom can be irrational, overwhelmed by emotion and unable to take decisive action.

- **The 'Guardian'.** The 'Guardian' protects the boundaries of the 'Kingdom' from invasion. This is the child's protective anger, that energy which enables them to keep themselves and others safe. The 'Guardian' is a warrior. This does not equate to aggression, but rather symbolises the ability to take action in defence of the 'Kingdom'. However, the 'Guardian's' counsel needs to be balanced by the 'empathy of the 'Bard' and the 'Guardian' should always act in service to the King otherwise their conclusions and advice may be harsh or even bullying.

- **The 'Court Scientist'.** This 'advisor' is concerned with facts and logic. This is the rational part of the child's interior world, the part which observes and evaluates the evidence. However, if the 'Court Scientist' is not tempered by the 'Bard', he, or she, can be somewhat cold and lacking in empathy.

So the 'King' must take the content of the story itself, whether you choose to read it or tell it to the child, and must consider the thoughts and ideas which emerge from the story in the light of counsel from the three 'advisors'; i.e. all the ideas and thoughts the child/children may generate in response to the story. If the story is being told 1:1 these can be interjected by the child at any time, in a class, or group setting it is best, for practical reasons, to gather the ideas after the story has been told. Any idea arising from the story can be categorised according to whether it is a 'Bard', 'Guardian' or 'Court Scientist' idea. There can be discussion regarding whether one idea needs to be balanced by input from another 'advisor'. If we take the example of the familiar story of the 'boy who cried wolf', the 'Bard' might argue that it is very sad that the boy came to such a terrible end because he must have been very lonely tending to the sheep all on his own. If he had friends with him, he wouldn't have had to lie. The 'Guardian', however, might say that the boy's fate was deserved because lying is wrong. The Court Scientist might be focused on finding a more efficient system for warning of wolf attacks! The task is to find an agreed response having considered all the perspectives. We should also remember not to take ourselves too seriously. There should always be a place in the King's court for the 'Jester' who punctures grandiosity. Storytelling should always be fun.

2. **The Royal decree:** Once the counsel of his advisors has been sought and the strengths and flaws of each idea considered, the 'King' issues a 'Royal Decree'. This takes the form of a generalisable principle which can then be re-applied in different context in a child's experience. When considering how to arrive at a principle it may be useful to consider the following simple formula: problem/ challenge + strategy/ solution = principle. In our example

of the story of the 'boy who cried wolf', the problem is that the boy develops a reputation as a liar, so when he is telling the truth, nobody believes him, with grave consequences. The Royal decree should not be specific to the events in the story, ie it should make no reference to wolves or the boy who cried wolf. The Royal Decree needs to be generalisable; a distillation of a challenge and its potential solution. If we again take 'the boy who cried wolf' as an example, following discussion, this might lead to a principle such as 'If I keep making the same mistake over and over, I may get a reputation which will be hard to shift. I should do my best to learn from my mistakes and change my actions'.

3. **Peace in the 'Kingdom':** The 'Royal Decree' is intended to make the 'Kingdom' a happier, more ordered place. For this to take effect, it will be necessary to find examples of where the 'decree' might be useful. This is the stage at which the child starts thinking and talking explicitly and directly about their own experience. How can they use the 'decree' in their own life, in their learning, in their friendships, at home etc.

In this collection, suggestions are offered following each story. A commentary is provided for each story entitled 'thinking about this story'. Suggestions are then given for encouraging 'the King's advisors' discussion, developing 'Royal Decree' principles and re-contextualising those principles in the 'Kingdom' of the child's experience. As with the 'Thinking about this story' commentaries, these suggestions are merely indicative examples and are in no way intended to be exhaustive. The intention is that you develop, with your child/ children real, personal and meaningful examples of your own.

Bruno the Truffle Hound

Bruno was a dog. More than that, he was a hound. Better still; a truffle hound. Bruno's master, Pierre, his father and his grandfather before that, were famous throughout the whole province as breeders and trainers of the very best truffle hounds. And truffles, as we know, are very valuable things.

Early each morning Bruno and his beloved master Pierre, would head out to the woods, before the flowers opened and joined with the other distracting smells of the day; pet dogs (which Bruno felt a little superior to), and delicious breakfast smells wafting through kitchen windows. Nothing in the world made Bruno happier than being in the woods with his master. Those mornings were just perfect. Bruno longed for the moment when Pierre would give the command and set him off in search of the prized truffles. He would follow his exceptional nose, moving swiftly, purposefully from tree to tree, seeking out the distinctive, heady aroma of the hidden gems buried in the rich earth below. But

this particular morning was different.

Exceptional in fact. Bruno walked with

Pierre from the farmhouse, his admiring

gaze fixed on his master as usual. They

entered the woods by the same route they

always did; through the old gate at the end

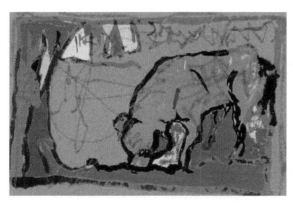 of the

lane, but

Pierre

decided

they would walk on to a place near the far

boundary of the family farm in order to

check the fences. Bruno was still a young dog and had never been there before, but he revelled in the delight of that extra hour spent walking in the woods by Pierre's side.

It was still early when they reached the spot. Pierre examined the fences and made a few repairs. Then it was Bruno's time to please his beloved Pierre.

'Find them Bruno! Find them!'.

Bruno made not a sound, but set about his task, his nose sweeping the woodland floor, dappled sun warm on his glossy, chocolate-brown coat. Sleek and shiny as a seal he moved amongst the Birch and Ash and Poplar of the woods. Then he froze, overwhelmed by the rich, earthy smell of the prize he sought. Bruno gave his signal bark, danced around the spot, then pawed the earth. Never before had the presence of the truffles been so overpowering. Pierre fussed over Bruno, tickling his ears and rubbing his chest vigorously.

'Good boy, Bruno, good dog, good dog!'

 Bruno was in heaven and felt he might burst with joy. Pierre took a small trowel from his canvas pack and began, carefully, to dig for the black treasure. Bruno looked on, eyes bright, panting excitedly. He knew this was extra-special. He couldn't wait to see Pierre's face when he uncovered them. Bruno had never smelled such an intoxicating abundance of truffles. There

were hundreds. He could smell them all.

Then Pierre reached the treasure, just a few inches below the dried leaves and moist mulch of the woodland floor.

'Good boy, Bruno, clever dog, good dog!'

Bruno was showered with ear-tickles and chest rubs before Pierre carefully placed three large, black truffles into the side pocket of his pack.

But then he stood up and began to walk away. Bruno barked. Why had his dear master stopped digging?

'Come on Bruno, let's go. Three in one dig. That's never happened before. An excellent start. Clever dog! '

Bruno was confused. Master must keep digging. Just a little further. Just a little deeper. He would be so happy. So happy.

'Bruno, let's go'.

Bruno barked his signal bark.

'Yes Bruno, good dog. We've got them. Now let's try somewhere else.

Bruno barked again and started digging at the spot.

'Bruno. Now. Let's go'.

Bruno was desperate that his master should have the joy of the abundance of truffles lying just below the surface. But he had never disobeyed, and master had called him. 'Bruno!' Pierre's voice was now harsh, and it cut straight to Bruno's heart, which felt like it would break. He must go to his master. He must obey.

 Bruno ran to his master's side.

'Good dog, Bruno. Good dog'. Pierre, reached down as he walked. Without looking, he ruffled Bruno's shoulders. Bruno's tail wagged, and his tongue lolled at the side of his mouth as he panted blissfully alongside his beloved master.

They continued searching all day long. They walked for many miles, stopping from time to time at Bruno's signal. Pierre dug

many shallow holes. Shallow because his

family had known for generations that

truffles only ever grow just below the

surface. Together they found four more

truffles that day. Pierre was pleased and

this made Bruno very happy. They never

did return to the spot at the far boundary

of the farm. And the truffles lie there still.

Hundreds of them.

Thinking about this story:

How do we motivate children to continue to invest effort when the going gets tough and the 'prize' seems intangible and beyond reach? This story offers a tantalising little vignette in which a prize, in great abundance, lies within reach, just a few more strokes of Pierre's trowel beneath the surface. Sometimes success really is down to perseverance; hanging in there just a little longer, even though it requires effort.

There are, of course, many alternative readings.

Children live in a world where the balance of power is usually quite heavily weighted towards teachers, parents and other adults. This can be a frustrating world for the child who often finds it difficult to get their voice heard. Bruno knows something important, something which he is aware would bring great happiness to his beloved Pierre, but he has no way of communicating this to his master. This imbalance in the power dynamic opens up an opportunity to discuss with children how it feels when they can't make their voice heard, or when the grown-ups don't recognise the importance of what they have to say. What of the tension between 'tradition' and flexibility? The story opens up a space for considering when it is important and beneficial to recognise that a parent, or teacher may know something the child does not know. In what circumstances might it be prudent to listen to the adult and accept their guidance?

Is it right that Pierre continues to do things the way they have always been done? Stability, consistency, security; these are all vital needs for a child. But it is through stretching and challenging ourselves that we arrive at meaning in our lives. How, then, can we help children to strike the correct balance between healthy risk-taking, which moves them to the next phase of their development, and appropriate caution, which keeps them safe; change and new ideas versus tried and tested ways of doing things?

Furthermore, is our value only to be found in pleasing others? This is an important consideration and a vital one on a child's journey to selfhood. A child's appreciation of their inherent value will aid them immeasurably in defending the boundaries of that selfhood.

'Attention-seeking' is a term which is often used negatively, even pejoratively, but all human beings, especially children have a fundamental and entirely appropriate need to give and receive attention. Bruno finds great joy in the attention he receives from Pierre, but it is also evident that his own attention is very much focused on his master. The gift of attention is a gift to be shared and without this precious exchange, we cannot thrive.

On a more subtle level, the story provides an opportunity to discuss the value of knowing what is 'enough'. Is the real prize in this tale not the truffles, but rather the bond of love which exists between Bruno and Pierre and the golden time they spend together in nature?

1. **'The King's advisors':**

'The Bard': Friendship, happiness, communication/ misunderstanding, contentment.

'The guardian': Frustration, perseverance/ not giving up just before finding your 'treasure' value, loyalty.

'The Court Scientist': Flexibility/ rigidity, familiarity/ novelty, How do we measure what is enough?

2. 'Royal Decree':

'Sometimes, when I feel like giving up, it helps to think that I'm 'nearly there' and success is just around the corner'.

'It can be frustrating when people don't listen, but if I stay calm and focus on what I can do, other people's behaviour doesn't have to affect me'.

'Sometimes, if I'm too 'stuck' in one way of doing things, I miss out. Its best to be flexible'.

'Getting more and more stuff isn't the best way to be happy. Happiness comes through my relationships with other people'.

'The best way to have good friends is to be a good friend'.

'Sometimes new things are scary, but it helps if I use the skills and knowledge I already have to help me in the new situation'.

'Sometimes, when it is something I really can't change, it helps me if I can accept things rather than trying to change them and getting frustrated'.

'Sometimes other people may know things I don't know and I can learn if I listen to them'.

3. 'Peace in the Kingdom':

This story has clear implications for inter-personal relationships and behaviour.

The idea of flexibility has applications academically as well as socially. Planning is essential for learning, but it can become an obstacle if the plan is too rigid. It is important to remain open to trying a different approach if the initial plan isn't working.

There is much value to be taken from an exploration of the idea of frustration. This can be approached, initially, by looking at the story. Firstly, the child can re-tell the story, with a particular focus on the sequence of events. Once this is done, the child can then start considering cause and effect. What led up to Bruno's frustration (what were the causes/ antecedents), how did the frustration manifest itself (the event), and what happened (the consequences). This template can then be used to explore frustrating events in the child's life. What happened in the lead up to the event, what happened, what were the consequences? The child can then use the skills developed when considering the sequence of events in the story to re-tell the story of their own frustrating event, perhaps adding a more positive and satisfying ending.

Folami and The Great Tree

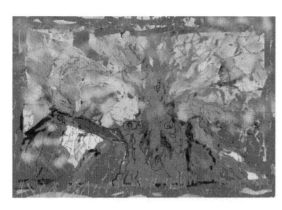 There were

three

things

everyone

knew about Folami; He wasn't a baby, (but

he wasn't a grown-up Chimpanzee either.

He was somewhere in between). He was

always worried that he and his family and

friends wouldn't get enough fruit to eat.

Most of the other young chimpanzees also

thought he was a bit of a bully.

In the land where Folami lived, there was a great fruit tree. The Great Tree stood exactly half way between the mountain and the river.

Some of the trees in the forest were tall and spindly, with dry, brittle branches and fierce sharp spines instead of leaves. They had dry seed cases which rattled when they fell to the ground. The Chimpanzees who lived in that land called these Ouch Trees.

Other trees were short and stumpy, with thick, spongy branches to store the water which fell in the rainy season. These had

succulent, rounded leaves full of moisture.

The Chimpanzees called these Juicy Trees.

The Ouch Trees stretched towards the sky,

way above the creatures that crawled on

the dry earth. These creatures; the lizards

and snakes and insects and little mice-like

creatures were grateful for the dappled

shade the trees provided. But the Great

Tree towered over all the other trees of

the forest.

Some of the other forest trees had fruit

which ripened in the spring or summer.

There were even a few which gave fruit in Autumn, but the fruit of the Great Tree was the most delicious in the whole forest, and what's more, in the winter, it was the only tree which had any fruit at all.

Now, the thing is, there were two tribes of Chimpanzees who lived in the forest; the River Tribe and the Mountain Tribe. The River Tribe were lean and muscular. They were fast and agile. Their fur was Reddish-brown.

The Mountain Tribe were big and powerful. They moved more slowly, but they were stronger than the River

Chimpanzees. Their arms were short and

strong. Their fur was the same reddish -

brown colour as the River Tribe but it was

denser, to keep them warm in the high,

cold mountains.

Both the River Chimpanzees and the

Mountain Chimpanzees had strong, sharp

teeth and they all really needed the fruit

from the Great Tree. Without it they would

go hungry in the winter and many just

wouldn't survive. That's how important

the Great Tree was. It was so serious for

both the Mountain Tribe and the River

Tribe that they used to have terrible fights

over the fruit of the Great Tree and

sometimes they would get badly hurt.

Folami, used to get very upset about all of

this. The truth is that he was scared. He

worried a lot that his family and his friends

 wouldn't

have enough

to eat. More

than anything

he worried about the Mountain Tribe. He

was ashamed `of being scared and used to

pretend he wasn't. He would snarl and

growl and push the younger River

Chimpanzees around to show them just

how tough he was. One day, Afolabi, the

Chief of the River Tribe looked down from

her place high in a tall Ouch Tree and saw

Folami snarling and pushing one of the

younger Chimpanzees. She told him off so

badly. 'What do you think you are doing? I

don't ever want to see you bullying the

young ones ever again. You should be

ashamed of your behaviour. It is

disgraceful'. Folami was really upset.

Didn't the Chief realise he was just showing everyone how strong he was so they would know he could protect them from the Mountain Chimpanzees?

Folami was so fed up and anxious. 'It's no use', he said to himself. 'I'll just have to leave the River Tribe and join the Mountain Tribe. Maybe they will want me.'

Folami was just setting off towards the mountain when he saw Adisa, the oldest, wisest Chimpanzee in the whole River tribe sitting calmly and contentedly by the River.

Folami was very fond of the old Chimpanzee and he didn't want to leave without saying goodbye. Old Adisa patted the dusty river bank with his right hand and Folami sat down beside him. Sure enough, Folami had soon blurted out the whole story. 'Hmmmm', said Old Adisa. 'I can see that you care very much about your friends and family. It seems to me that you are a very kind and caring Chimpanzee. I also think you are a very frightened Chimpanzee. You know, Folami. It's ok to be scared. We all feel scared sometimes. Do you really want to join the Mountain Tribe?'

'Not really', said Folami. 'I would miss everybody so much.' He was, I have to say, already feeling very sad because he had lost some of his best friends because of all the snarling and growling and pushing. It didn't seem to make any difference that he was only trying to show them how strong he was and how good he would be at scaring the Mountain Chimpanzees.

'Ah, I see', said wise Old Adisa. 'I think we need to make a plan'. They whispered

 together late into the night hatching a very clever plan.

Early next morning there was a great commotion in the camp of the River Tribe. The Mountain Tribe were on their way to raid the Great Tree. There was going to be a terrible fight over the fruit. Someone was sure to get badly hurt.

The River Chimpanzees nervously took their places to defend the Great Tree. They could see the dust clouds rising in the morning sun as the Mountain Tribe drew nearer and nearer. The atmosphere was very tense and they trembled, holding their breath, waiting for the terrible battle to begin.

Suddenly two figures appeared out of the dust between the River Tribe and the Mountain Tribe. The River Chimpanzees gasped when they realised it was their very own Folami. But he wasn't alone. Standing majestically beside him was Khari the Lion, King and ruler over all the land between the River and the Mountain. He spoke in a powerful, commanding voice.

'This clever young Chimpanzee has explained everything. I now understand this difficult problem and I have made a decision. There will be no more fighting between the River Tribe and the Mountain Tribe. The Great Tree has plenty of fruit for all of you'.

This is what King Khari decided. The River Tribe would have all the fruit on the North side of the Great Tree and the Mountain Tribe would have all the fruit on the South side of the Great Tree. King Khari's word was final. There was no more fighting between the Mountain Tribe and the River Tribe, and in time some of them even became friends and shared their fruit.

Folami became a hero, respected by the whole tribe. Chief Afolabi gave him a special title; 'Folami the Wise'. His friends and family were very proud of him, and when he grew up, he even became the Chief of the River Tribe himself, and a great Chief he was. He kept the River Tribe safe and happy and became a good friend of the Chief of the Mountain Chimpanzees.

The Great Tree continued to feed them all for many, many years...... and I'm told it still does to this day.

Thinking about this story:

The story of the Great Tree provides many opportunities for comparison, categorisation and ranking according to different criteria. It encourages thinking about friendship, belonging and loyalty. What does it mean to be a friend? How should friends behave towards one another? What do true strength and courage look like? It also offers a springboard for exploring the idea of peaceful and appropriate conflict resolution. Many children grow up exposed to their parent's or carer's anxieties around financial insecurity. This story presents a powerful template which encourages a mindset of hope and optimism which counteracts the crippling effects of fear and anxiety. All will be well if wisdom and kindness are employed to resolve differences.

The pressure on children to conform to the expectations of their peer group is enormous. The harsh world of social media projects brutal and unrelenting messages onto the child about how they 'should' be if they want to belong. As a result, children are sometimes tempted to align themselves with behaviours and attitudes which are not congruent with what they really believe. Such is the power of the legitimate human need to feel connected to a community.

Folami's meeting with wise old Adisa is replete with potential meaning, Folami does not act immediately upon his impulse to leave the River tribe, he first consults with wise Adisa. The development of the ability to restrain impulsivity is immensely empowering for a child and has far reaching social, emotional and academic implications. The child who can stop and consider the potential consequences of a given course of action is freed from the tyranny of automated, impulsive reactive behaviour and experiences their own ability to impose order on their internal world and make conscious, volitional choices.

1. 'The King's advisors':

'The Bard': 'friendship', 'sharing', 'diversity', 'belonging', 'co-operation'.

'The Guardian': 'bullying', 'racism/ discrimination', 'feeling safe and secure', 'responsibility', 'black and white thinking', 'sticking to your own values'.

'The Court Scientist': 'looking for similarities and differences', 'advice' (advice is an interesting topic for discussion; is it based on good information/ evidence? Who is qualified to give advice?), 'wisdom' again we should consider whether wisdom only arrives once the King/ Queen/ Sovereign has considered the counsel of the advisors and reached a balanced conclusion).

2. 'Royal Decree':

'If I get better at stopping, thinking and comparing consequences before acting, my choices will be better'.

''Real friends will accept me for who I am'.

'Bullies are often afraid. If I am afraid, I should ask for help'.

'Things aren't always the way I think they are. It helps if I don't jump to conclusions'.

'I should listen to my own feelings about what is right and wrong, even when it is difficult'.

3. 'Peace in the Kingdom':

The social context in which children live has become exponentially more complex, particularly with the advent of social media. The pressure to conform has always existed, but the ludicrous, artificial standards of appearance to which a child is expected to compare themselves are highly nuanced and often deeply destructive. Likewise, bullying has always existed, but its mechanisms and its dark strategies have changed. Mobile devices along with pressure on the child to be connected at all times in the same way as their peers now allows the bullies access to every area of the child's life, every hour of the day.

In the story, the powerful, irresistible need to belong, to be part of a group, lead Folami to abandon his 'tribe' in the hope of being accepted. The 'tribe' can be viewed literally as the people of significance around the child, or metaphorically as all the beliefs, characteristics and values which constitute the child, and which can be 'abandoned' in the face of the powerful need for acceptance. Folami's thinking is clearly very 'black and white', either or'. Children often need help in identifying 'shades of grey' and the story offers a pattern whereby a 'black and white' reaction to the problem is tempered and adapted with the introduction of a wise and balanced

perspective. The principles emerging in

the 'Royal decree' can, therefore, be

'bridged' to the child's own experience of

feeling excluded or indeed of excluding

others.

Stubborn Stripes

Once, long ago in the far-off foothills of the

mighty Himalayas, there lived a tiger cub

named Stripes. He wasn't a baby tiger, but

he wasn't a magnificent adult tiger either.

He was still quite little.

 One day, a

venerable

old tiger

came to visit

Stripes and

his family in

their deep

jungle home. The rain started to fall just as the old tiger began to recount the tale of his long journey to visit them. The noise of the rain on the leaves made it difficult to hear, but they all listened intently to the old tiger's tale of adventure.

Now, it's quite a sad thing in a way, and not easy to talk about, but it has to be said anyway. You may or may not know that a tiger's very favourite thing to eat is the deer who wander the great forests of Asia. Now deer are beautiful creatures, and it would be lovely if they didn't have to be eaten by any creature, but tigers do have to eat too after all. Well, as you can imagine, the whole family listened with special interest when the old tiger reached the point in his story where he spoke of seeing hundreds of plump, delicious deer wandering in the part of the forest where the trees are tallest.

The very next morning, Stripes and his family set off to find that herd of deer because they were all very hungry. They travelled for two whole days along the rough trails of the forest until they came to

 a fork in the track. Sitting on a branch, high on a tree next to the fork in the road, was a big owl. 'Where do these tracks lead?' asked Stripes, without so much as a please or a good morning. 'Well', said the owl, 'This path leads to the part of the forest where the trees are tallest, and this path leads to where the trees are smallest. Well, of course, Stripes charged off without even a backwards glance. 'Where on earth are

you going in such a rush?' said his big

sister, 'I'm going to be first to eat some

juicy deer' said Stripes. 'Well you're going

the wrong way', replied his sister, 'because

they are in the part of the forest where the

trees are tallest, old tiger said so'. 'No he

didn't, he said smallest', complained

Stripes indignantly. 'He definitely said

tallest', replied the others, all at once. 'No,

he did not, no he did not', shouted Stripes

furiously. Little Stripes argued and argued,

insisting he was right. He refused to budge,

and finally stomped off grumpily down the

path to where the trees are smallest. The others gave up trying to convince him and headed off in the opposite direction.

After a long, lonely time, Stripes reached the part of the forest where the trees are smallest. It wasn't a very nice place. The trees were tiny and sad looking. They had no fruit or flowers on them and there were no animals anywhere. Still little Stripes stuck to thinking that he was right and the old tiger had said that this was the place. He searched and searched for hours and got hungrier and hungrier until his tummy growled like the biggest tiger you could

ever imagine.

 Meanwhile,
the others
had reached
the part of

the forest where the trees are tallest and,

sure enough, there were deer everywhere,

more than they had ever seen. Soon they

were having a great feast.

By now little Stripes was very, very hungry,

and really, really lonely. He flopped down

by a tiny tree and felt like crying. Just then,

the wise owl flew by and landed on a spindly branch right above him. 'Hello Stripes', he said, 'What are you doing here?' (although he knew exactly why Stripes was there....he was just being kind). 'I just flew past the part of the forest where the trees are tallest. Your whole family are there, feasting on deer'. Stripes realised that he had been wrong. Very, very wrong. He had mis-heard the old tiger because of the rain, and now his stubbornness had made him very hungry and very sad. 'Follow me', said the owl, 'I'll

lead you to them, it's not so far'.

Stripes was more than a little bit

embarrassed when he finally reached his

family, but he knew he had to be more

grown-up than ever before, and that's

exactly what he did. 'Sorry I was so

stubborn, I got it wrong. I mis-heard the

old tiger, you were right all along. I'm

going to listen more carefully from now

on'. 'That's ok Stripes', said the others, all

in one big, warm, welcoming voice. 'We've

saved plenty for you. Come and join the

feast'. Little Stripes wasn't so stubborn after that, and he never went hungry again.

Thinking about this story:

In common with many others in this collection, this story can be approached on many levels. It provides an opportunity to explore important thinking skills such as directing your focus and attention appropriately, gathering information effectively, the importance of planning, and crucially, the importance of remaining flexible in the event that a plan needs to be changed. Stripes is faced with a choice when he reaches a fork in the road. What do we base our choices on? Are our 'choices' automatic, impulsive reactions, or are they based on comparison of the potential consequences of each course of action. Impulsivity is a major source of problems for children and this story is a great springboard for further work on the essential thinking skills of restraint of impulsivity and comparison as the basis for making good choices.

The dilemma of the needs of the deer versus the needs of the tiger is an interesting one. The needs of different parties are not always compatible. How do we reach compromise?

On another level, the story provides a safe forum in which to explore the idea of letting go of ideas, ways of thinking and behaviours which are not helpful to the child. This must be approached with care and sensitivity. While it may be of great benefit to a child to be able to let go, forgive and move on regarding a petty feud with a classmate, the adult must, of course, remain alert at all times to any genuine bullying, harm, neglect or even abuse which the child may be experiencing and act promptly and in accordance with child protection protocols. The story of Stripes offers to create stability in a child's world by embedding a message that, even when a mistake is made, even when they behave inappropriately, they are still acceptable and lovable. This message is particularly important for the child who may not experience such acceptance and love in their daily life. The template

offered by the story shows an alternative

reality. Such a child may, of course, need

additional support to believe in this

alternative.

1. 'The King's advisors':

'The Bard': 'mistakes', 'humility',

'forgiveness', 'kindness', 'admitting a

mistake and saying sorry'.

'The Guardian': 'making good decisions',

'letting go and moving on', 'being

stubborn/ sticking up for yourself' (are these always the same thing?).

'The Court Scientist': 'focus and attention', 'good information gathering', 'being wise' (it could be argued that wisdom only arrives once the King/ Queen/ Sovereign has reflected on the counsel of their advisors and reached a balanced decision).

2. **'Royal Decree':**

'Sometimes a very small mistake can cause a big problem'

'Many mistakes can be corrected if I change my attitude and have humility'.

'The longer I persist with a mistake, the harder it gets to correct it'.

'Making mistakes is normal. It doesn't change who I am'.

'If I say sorry, I should take responsibility for my mistake and ask how I can make amends'.

'If I carefully compare potential consequences, I'll make better decisions'.

'When I have an important decision to make, sometimes it helps to ask for help'.

3. 'Peace in the Kingdom':

When children behave in a manner which the adults may perceive as 'difficult', or 'challenging', 'disrespectful', or ''disobedient', what we are often seeing is the manifestation of a mistake; a poor decision rooted in impulsivity and under-developed skills in comparison and consideration of consequences. This is further complicated when we consider that many of these under-developed thinking skills are, in turn, rooted in

distress and trauma. Many children are so

anxious, they simply can't think clearly. As

adults we have a fundamental duty to

develop safety for the children in our care.

If we don't meet this foundational need in

our children, all learning and development;

academic, social and emotional, will be

stunted. But so often, not only do we fail

to recognise that we be falling short of

fulfilling our duty to create safety, we

punish children for manifesting their

distress through their behaviour and interactions.

The acceptance of mistakes implicit in this story provides a way in to exploring the causes/ antecedents of mistakes and the consequences of those mistakes, not with a view to punishing or shaming those mistakes, but to strengthen the child's capacity to impose order on their thinking, their emotions and their behaviour. If the child knows that humility does not equate to humiliation, the road is opened to the correction of behaviour which harms.

The Cub Who Grew up Safe and Sound

Once upon a time there was a pride of

lions. There was a mummy lion and a

daddy lion and a little lion cub. One day

the daddy lion went away and the rain

didn't fall for weeks. The grass couldn't

grow without the rain, so the zebras, and

gazelles and antelopes had nothing to eat.

 This meant

that they all

had to go

away

somewhere else to look for food. Well, you probably know what lions eat. Yes, that's right, they eat zebras and gazelles and antelopes. So things were pretty bad. The mummy lion just couldn't find enough food for her cub. She just couldn't look after him properly, even though she really wanted to.

This is what she did. She knew there were two very special people who lived in the village. They were both very kind and very clever and they loved to look after lost and injured animals. They were very good at it.

The mummy lion decided to take her little lion to these good people where he would be safe and have everything he needed, especially lots of love. She was so hungry herself that she couldn't show much love for the lion cub. She was very sad, but she left him in the village and went to try to find food for herself because she was starving.

You can imagine how surprised the two people from the village were to find a cute, little lion cub on their doorstep.....surprised and delighted. They had always wanted a little lion to care for.

They loved him straight away. They gave

him lots of good food to eat and lots and

lots of love.But the lion cub didn't know

how to live in a house and he used to tear

up the carpets, bite the furniture and

generally make a terrible mess.

 Bath-times were

particularly

chaotic. He didn't

know how to

have a bath, but

he really needed one because he was

getting a bit smelly and none of the other little creatures wanted to play with him.

He made a terrible, wet mess at first, but he was still loved. He had very sharp little teeth and claws and sometimes he would hurt the people who loved him, not because he wanted to, but just because he hadn't yet learned how to be with people. He even hurt the other little creatures sometimes. Again, this wasn't because he wanted to hurt them, he just didn't know how to play properly, or how to have fun. Nobody had shown him (the mummy and daddy lion had been too cross and hungry to teach him these things). But the two kind and clever people who loved him very much, really knew how to teach him, and he soon learned how to play.

They also taught him how to eat from a bowl without making a terrible commotion. He learned how to have a bath without drowning the whole bathroom and he learned how to play and laugh and make friends. Some days he would spend happy hours running and jumping with his new friends. He started to feel much happier. He was careful not to

hurt the people he loved, or the other little

creatures with his sharp teeth and claws.

In time he grew to be a big, strong lion,

and a very fine lion he was.

 One night,
when the
two, kind
people were

asleep, the lion heard a strange sound. He

looked outside and he saw two fierce

hyenas trying to get into the house. Now

hyenas could be very dangerous to those

two, kind people. The lion burst through the door and let out a deep, powerful RRRRRROOOOAAAAARRRRRR!!!!!!!! The hyenas were terrified and ran away never to return. The little lion cub, who was now a full-grown, brave, magnificent lion had saved the day. He was a hero. The two, kind people knew he was ready to return to the wild, and though he was sad to go, he knew it was time too. He walked off, proud and strong, early one morning, but every so often, he returned to the village to make sure everyone was safe and to

keep those hyenas away.

Thinking about this story:

Families take many different forms.

Children have an entirely legitimate need

to feel accepted and valued and this story

confirms the value of diversity with regard

to what constitutes the family unit and

opens the door to discussion of the

different forms family takes.

The legitimate need to belong is present in

all children, but the adopted child can

experience great challenge and insecurity

in this regard, often borne of interruptions

in bonding and attachment they cannot

consciously remember. The child's inner

turmoil may manifest in behaviour which

challenges the adults around them. Story

can, again, sneak past the guards at the

gate, past the defences which the child has

set up in their search for safety. Story can

reach within the child and offer them a

way of resolving the conflict. Adverse

childhood experiences or traumatic events

in childhood can change, in an instant, the

way a child responds to the world. If a child is provided with a safe, nurturing environment, healing moments can occur in an instant too.

1. **'The King's Advisors':**

'The Bard': Sadness, feeling overwhelmed, trusting safe adults, asking for help/ telling trusted adults how you are feeling.

'The Guardian':

Getting enough exercise, dealing with difficult 'angry' feelings. Using words not force to get needs met.

'The Court Scientist': Solving problems 'together' works better than struggling alone'.

2. 'Royal Decree':

'Feelings can be very complicated and its ok to ask for help'.

'I am loved and accepted even when I make mistakes'.

'Sometimes grown-ups will disapprove of my behaviour, but that doesn't mean they disapprove of me'.

'I will never feel better by making others feel bad'. 'If I help other children to feel safe and happy, I will feel safe and happy'.

3. 'Peace in the Kingdom':

What does it mean to belong? What 'feeling words' does the child associate with belonging? Charts, pictures, collages etc can be made to show all the different groups and communities to which a child belongs. It can be a very fruitful exercise to take each of the identified groups and consider both what we bring to the group and what we get from being part of the group. Are there groups we'd like to be

part of? What action can we take to move

towards that?

The little hippo who learned

Once upon a time, a wide, shallow river ran through the parched plains of the Serengeti in Africa, and by that river lived a little hippopotamus. He loved to roll around in the thick, gloopy mud on the banks of the great river. He also loved to play in the cool, clear water of the river and drink his fill. But most of all he loved to eat the long, juicy grass that grew along the banks of the river a little way downstream.

One day he was playing in the mud when his mum said, 'Hurry up now, it's time to cool off in the river and wash off some of that mud'. The little hippo was having so much fun that that he didn't want to leave. 'Just a

few more minutes, just a few more minutes', he complained.

After a long. Long time, and lots of reminders, he eventually got out of the mud. He was just about to jump into the inviting, cool, refreshing water when his mum shouted 'STOP!!!'. He looked down into the clear, sparkling water and was

shocked to see that it was full of hungry

crocodiles. He had to stay muddy for ages

and ages while he waited for the

crocodiles to go away. By the time they

left, the mud had dried hard and crusty on

his back and it took lots of scrubbing and

lots of time before it finally washed off.

'Oh well', said the little hippo, 'At least I'll

have lots of yummy grass to eat when I'm

finished here'. 'Hurry up now', said the

mummy hippo. 'You've been in there for

such a long time'. 'Just a few more

minutes, just a few more minutes', said

the little hippo.

 After ages and ages, and even more reminders, the little hippo finally got out of the water,

but when he arrived downstream at the

place where the delicious grass grew, he

couldn't get near it because the elephants

had arrived and wouldn't let him in. By the

time they had gone, most of the grass was

eaten, and the rest was squashed flat. The

little hippo went to bed very hungry that night.

The next morning, the little hippo was wallowing in the mud pool just like he always did. 'Time to get out', said mummy hippo....and WHOOSH!!! – the little hippo was out of the mud like a shot and straight into the river with a huge SPLAAAAASHH! (The crocodiles were still asleep you see).

 The mud washed off his back

easily and, after a short while, mummy hippo said, 'Time to get out', and WHOOOSH!!!- little hippo was out of the river in a flash and soon he was feasting on yummy, juicy grass. The elephants were still wallowing in the mud. Little hippo fell asleep that night with a lovely full tummy.

Thinking about this story:

It's such a familiar scenario. It can be parent to child, teacher to child, child to child, or even adult to adult. We want someone to do something, because we know it is in their interest to do it, but still they resist. We know there will likely be a consequence to that resistance, but to communicate that in a convincing and effective manner often seems impossible. This story, again, addresses the issue obliquely, through metaphor. A simple, but clear cause and effect pattern is presented which the child can then refer to when the occasion, inevitably, arises.

1. 'The King's Advisors':

'The Bard': Missing out, not getting what I need.

'The Guardian': Changing action, changing outcomes, being responsible, the purpose of 'rules', time and punctuality.

'The Court Scientist': Cause and consequence.

2. 'Royal Decree':

'I'm in charge of my behaviour, it's not in charge of me'

'Sometimes the grown-ups know things we don't'

'Sometimes rules are there to keep us safe'

'If I keep doing the same thing, I'll keep getting the same result'

'If there is something important to do, I need to plan enough time to do it'

3. 'Peace in the Kingdom':

Are there times when it is better to forego a short-term reward in favour of a greater long-term benefit? This is another story which allows for a discussion of volitional action based on thinking rather than impulsive, automated reactions based purely on emotion and gratification.

Conversely, there are times when prompt action is appropriate and indeed necessary. Once I know what needs to be done, I need to take action.

The connection between action and consequence (positive or negative) is often not clear or obvious, particularly to the young child. Here we have an illustration which is contained enough to show this connection in a manner accessible to the child. Similarly, the young child's experience and perception of time is less bounded and compartmentalised than the older child or adult. The story provides a 'way in' to discussing time. How is time measured? Are these measures natural; day/ night, seasons, lunar months etc, or are they artificial; seconds, minutes, hours etc. How is the child's day marked and boundaried? (e.g. breakfast, start of school day, playtime, lunch, morning/ afternoon etc)On a more subtle level, perhaps with older children, this can lead to a discussion about other boundaries which are natural and artificial. Natural boundaries such as mountain ranges or rivers have often, in time become national boundaries. We have divided the world into time zones for practical purposes. The conversation can become increasingly abstract with the discussion of categories, criteria for establishing categories and why we put things in categories. Is it always helpful? Can putting things, especially people, in categories cause problems? These are big, complex ideas, but children can think about big ideas provided they are presented in an accessible manner.

Let me be in charge

Once upon a time, long ago and in a far-off

land, there was a little boy. He lived in a

great, walled city with fine houses, paved

streets and even a great palace. In the

centre of this handsome city was a

wonderful market place where the people

would go to buy their food and all the

other things they could ever need, like

shoes, and clothes and pots and pans and

carpets, oil for their lamps, tables, chairs,

baskets.....well, you get the idea.

The market was always very busy, but everybody seemed to find what they were looking for. The little boy's mum and dad had a stall in the market where they sold very nice pots and pans. They made a good living, because everybody needs pots and pans. Their stall had been a great success for a very long time.

The little boy used to nag and nag and nag his parents to let him look after the stall.

'Please let me be in charge, please let me be in charge' he would say, but mum and dad said he was too young and it was the grown-ups who needed to be in charge because they knew how to run the stall properly.

One day, mum and dad had to go on a journey to visit a relative who wasn't very well. The little boy begged them to let him be in charge of the stall while they were away and, although they weren't sure about it, they agreed. He promised to do everything just the way he had seen them do it.

He felt very proud on that first day, standing at his stall, surrounded by shiny pots and pans, but it didn't take long before he got a little bit bored because nobody was buying anything. He had a look around the stall. 'I know what I'll do' he said, 'I'll just re-arrange things a bit to make the stall more exciting. This is so dull. My way will be much more exciting, and people will buy lots of things. Mum and dad will be really pleased'. And with that he started re-organising everything;

moving big stacks of pots and pans, re-

arranging the whole stall. He thought

everything would be so much better if

everybody just did things his way. Just

when he was nearly finished making his

changes, a terrible thing happened. A

great, big, enormous pot....the biggest one

on the whole stall, wibbled and wobbled

and finally toppled from where he had

perched it on top of a huge stack of pots

and pans (he had put it there to attract

people's attention.....and it certainly did).

The great, big, enormous pot tumbled to

the ground with such a clatter that the

lady at the next stall, who had just bought

a huge pile of plates,

dropped every, single one of them, with an

almighty CRASH!!!!!!!   The man in the

 stall next to

the plate stall

was a

blacksmith

and he was

making shoes

for horses when the plates crashed down.

He got such a fright that he bashed his

thumb with his hammer and let out a huge

AIYEEEEEE!!!!!!

 His scream

was so loud

that it

terrified the

poor horses waiting for their horseshoes.

There were five of them and they all

reared up and whinnied and bolted. They

knocked over stalls and smashed tables as

they went. Soon the whole market was in

chaos, with horses and screaming

shoppers running around and stalls

collapsing, plates smashing and baskets

emptying their contents all over the place.

It was so noisy that the King could hear the

commotion all the way from the great hall

in his palace. The King and his Ministers

 panicked

because they

thought the

city was being

invaded. The

generals were summoned and the army

charged off to defend the city gates.

It was at this point that the little boy's mum and dad arrived back from their journey. The entire city was in a terrible mess. The market was empty and in tatters. All the people had been cleared off the streets by the army and told to stay indoors because the city was being invaded and there was going to be a great battle. But, of course, there was no invasion and there was no battle.

When the little boy's mum and dad got back to their house, they found the boy sitting nervously in the living room. 'What on earth happened in the market today?'

they gasped. 'I'm really not sure', said the

boy, 'I was just doing a little bit of re-

arranging'.

Thinking about this story:

Deferring gratification and the restraint of

impulsivity are major challenges of

childhood. When a child really wants

something, it can become all consuming.

Telling a child that the thing they really

want is not appropriate or reasonable, or

that they will have to wait, while

sometimes necessary, is likely to be met

with frustration and a degree of resentment. The above story offers a way in, under the radar. The child may identify with the protagonist's legitimate need to experience a sense of autonomy and control, but the story also demonstrates that, while the need is legitimate, the strategy employed to get the need met is inappropriate and the consequences ultimately destructive and troublesome. We should not underestimate the importance of nurturing an understanding that we all have a range of legitimate emotional needs, but that those needs must be met appropriately and in balance, or else they will impact on our ability to get other important needs met. In this case, the protagonist's drive to meet his need for control and autonomy ultimately impacts upon his need, and the needs of his family, for safety and security.

This story may also contain some gold for the child who is prone to obsessive, compulsive, anxiety driven thinking. Such a child will often feel a disproportionate sense of their own responsibility for making sure everything and everybody is

ok. The message that it is not our

responsibility, or indeed our right to be in

charge of everything may provide

reassurance for the anxious child.

1. **'The King's Advisors':**

'The Bard': frustration/ not getting what

you want, panic, misunderstandings,

impulsivity.

'The Guardian': making changes,

responsibility, control, status, competence.

'The Court Scientist': restraining impulsivity/ being patient

2. 'Royal Decree:

'Some things are the responsibility of adults'.

'Sometimes I will need support to achieve new things'.

'It's important to gather information before acting'.

'There is no need to change a plan if it is working well'.

'Just because I want something doesn't mean it's good for me to have it'.

3. 'Peace in the Kingdom:

Children, as with all human beings, have a legitimate need to experience a sense of control and autonomy in their lives. The journey to finding a balance in this regard is often a troublesome one. The need is legitimate, but the need must be met in balance and the strategies employed to get those needs met are often inappropriate. This story opens the door to discussion of the things it is appropriate for a child to have control of and those

which should remain the domain and

responsibility of adults.

The Wrong Job

Once upon a time there was a troop of monkeys who lived in the high trees of the deepest part of the jungle. They had everything they needed. They had fruit to eat, they drank the fresh water which collected in the leaves when it rained, and the young monkeys had lots of friends to play with and branches to climb on.

There was one particular young monkey called Basil. He wasn't a baby monkey, but he wasn't grown up either.

 Sometimes he did really grown-up, sensible things, but sometimes he did things that weren't grown-up and sensible at all. He was still learning.

Every day, first thing in the morning, while the monkeys were having their breakfast, the chief monkey would gather them all together to remind them of something very important (especially important for the young ones who were still learning). Basil didn't like the chief's speeches. He thought they were boring. Basil just

wanted to be like the strong guardian

monkeys who protected everybody. But

the chief's speeches were important. 'I

want to remind you of something very

important', she would say. 'Oh no, not

again' Basil would mutter grumpily to

himself. But the chief would carry on in her

strong, clear voice, 'We must never go

down to the bottom of the trees and walk

on the earth. There are many dangers

there. We must stay safe in the branches,

where the guardian monkeys can protect

us'. She said much the same thing every morning, 'We all have our special jobs to do; some of us collect water. Some of us collect fruit. The guardian monkeys protect us, and the young monkeys play and learn'.

One day, Basil and his friends were playing, chasing each other all around the high branches, when all of a sudden, they saw 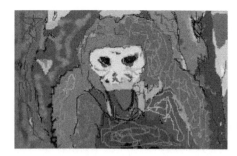 movements far below.

To their amazement, they saw two monkeys even

younger than them playing right at the bottom of the tree. Basil knew this was against the rules and he told his friends they should all go down and tell the young monkeys off. That's what a guardian monkey would do. They dashed to the bottom of the tree and grabbed the young monkeys. Soon a big commotion had started. Basil got into a nasty squabble with one of the younger monkeys and they were all so caught up in the argument that they didn't notice a dark shape closing in behind them.

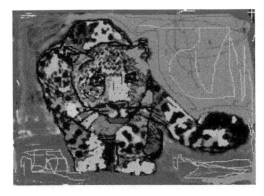 At the very last second, Basil turned and screamed as a huge leopard sprang towards them. All they could see was his huge, pointy teeth and the flash of his razor-sharp claws. Basil froze to the spot, too frightened to even move. Just as the leopard's huge, crushing paw was about to swipe Basil, a guardian monkey grabbed him and whisked him off, high into the branches.

Basil had had a very narrow escape, and so had his friends. The chief was furious. 'Is it your job to tell the young monkeys off? NO IT IS NOT!!!', she shouted. 'I am very, very cross with you. You are NOT a guardian monkey! It is the job of the guardian monkeys to protect us. It is NOT your job!'

Basil was very upset indeed.

A few days later, Basil was sitting on his own on one of the high branches feeling rather sad, when something caught his eye. Far below, one of the young monkeys, hardly more than a baby, had dropped a big, juicy orange and had climbed all the

way to the bottom of the tree to get it.

Basil was just about to dash down to tell

the little monkey off when he

remembered the chief's words. He quickly

climbed up to the highest branch in the

tree, where the Captain of the guardian

monkeys was keeping lookout. Basil

quickly explained to her what was

happening and the guardian monkeys all

sped off to the rescue. They got there just

in time because two big, hungry leopards

were prowling around the tree. One of

them was ready to pounce on the little monkey when the guardian monkeys arrived and managed to chase it away. The other leopard had sneaked almost to the top of the tree (leopards are very good climbers too), but the guardian monkeys spotted him and screeched and shook the branches and threw sticks and fruit until the leopard ran away.

Basil was a hero. Not only had his sharp eyes and quick thinking saved the little monkey, but if he hadn't alerted the guardian monkeys, the other leopard would have climbed right to the top of the tree and everyone would have been in danger.

Basil received a special award from the chief and when he grew up, he did become the Captain of the guardian monkeys and he still keeps the whole troop safe, right up to today.

Thinking about this story:

Hierarchies often seem unfair, particularly to children (it should be noted that hierarchies are sometimes unjust). But children can also recognise the utility of

hierarchies. The child can readily see the

chaos that would ensue if, for example,

the reception class were put in charge of

the school. The focus here can centre on

the criteria used for assigning hierarchies.

Are they appropriate? Are they just?

1. **'The King's Advisors':**

'The Bard': Being misunderstood, good

intentions,

'The Guardian': Shared, universal duties and responsibilities versus specific duties and responsibilities. Why do different people have different 'jobs'? Talents, abilities, qualities, values (what makes me 'me'?) Being 'in charge' of your own feelings and actions.

'The Court Scientist': Hierarchies, 'power'. Who should be 'in charge'?

2. 'Royal Decree':

'Sometimes I may do the wrong thing when I'm actually trying to help. If this happens, it's best to stay calm. I am still acceptable and lovable'

'I can be 'in charge' of my own feelings and behaviour'

'Grown-ups have to be in charge of some things to keep us all safe'

'If I make a mistake, then change my thinking and behaviour, I can make amends for the mistake'

3. 'Peace in the Kingdom':

Ranking and hierarchies can only exist through a process of comparison. Comparison should be based on appropriate criteria. Comparison can then form the basis of categorisation, and categorisation in turn providers the basis for analogical reasoning (e.g horse is to stable as dog is to......kennel). This story contains scope for valuable exploration with regard to all of these foundational thinking skills. Furthermore, these thinking skills are invaluable in their contribution to the child's perception of stability and

predictability in the world, so essential for

emotional security and resilience.

The Donkey Princess

There was once a King and a Queen who had a beautiful baby girl. She seemed just perfect in every way. But one day, the wicked wizard from the deep, dark forest on the edge of the Kingdom came, and because he was so jealous of how happy the King and Queen were, he waved his magic wand and put a spell on the little Princess. This is what he said;

'When the Princess is 8 years old, she will begin to turn into a donkey, with great, big, donkey teeth, two long ears and a swishy donkey tail.....ha, ha, ha, ha!!!!! With that horrible cackle, he disappeared in a puff of smelly, green smoke.

The King and Queen were very upset and cried and cried. Then they sent messengers out all over the Kingdom to try to find a solution and to stop this terrible thing from happening. But nobody knew what to do.

The years passed and the beautiful little Princess began to grow up. Still nobody could find a solution. Some people suggested she should stand on her head. Some said she should dress like a boy, some said she should paint her face purple. But, of course, none of the suggestions worked, until, just before her 8th birthday, a wise old witch arrived at the palace. These were her instructions;

'I know how to stop the Princess turning into a donkey, and I've arrived not a moment too soon, for tomorrow she will be 8 years old and the spell will begin to work. This is what you must do; every morning, early in the morning, she must walk down to the lake at the far end of the palace gardens. Since ancient times this has been a magical place. If your daughter washes her face each morning in the enchanted waters, she will grow into a wise, beautiful and brave Princess.

Well, as you can imagine, the King and Queen were overjoyed. They thanked the wise witch and explained everything carefully to the little Princess. Now everything was fine for a while, but it was a long walk to the magic lake, especially when winter came. The little Princess didn't like leaving her cozy, warm bed early in the morning to walk through the frosty garden, all the way to the icy waters of the lake. Even once she had dragged herself out of bed, what she really wanted to do was have fun with her friends, not make the lonely, cold walk to the lake. She started to get very grumpy about the whole thing, and one morning she refused to go altogether. She just curled up under her warm, goose-feather quilt and went back to sleep.

After a while, she did crawl out of bed and got dressed. She was bored and wanted to play with her friends. She went into her bathroom to brush her teeth but when she looked in the mirror, what do you think she saw? To her horror, she saw a row of big, donkey teeth grinning back at her from the end of a long, donkey snout. 'This is terrible!' she screamed as she ran from the room to find the King and Queen. It was a cold day, so she grabbed her hat from the hook by the door, but when she tried to pop it on her head, it wouldn't fit. I'm sure you can guess why. Yes. She had sprouted two, long, donkey ears. She was so shocked that she had to sit down, but when she tried, she couldn't fit on the chair.....yes, she had grown a long, swishy, donkey tail. The Donkey Princess rushed to the King and Queen, who immediately bundled her into the royal carriage and sped towards the magic lake. Now they didn't just wash her face, I can tell you. No, the King grabbed her arms and the Queen grabbed her feet and after a couple of practice swings, they plunged her right into the lake. This was a good idea because, sure enough, as soon as she emerged from the water, although she was dripping wet and freezing, she didn't have a tail, or donkey ears, or donkey teeth. You can rest assured that, after her shock, she never again refused to get out of bed

early, and she never again complained

about the walk to the magic lake.

 After some time, as luck would have it, the wicked old wizard died (an

angry elephant passing through the deep,

dark forest had sat on him). The spell was

broken. The Princess did grow up to be

wise, and beautiful and strong. In time she

became a just and brave Queen and ruled

over a happy, prosperous kingdom for many years.

Thinking about this story:

It is often a challenge to get young children to do the things we, as adults, think are self-evidently, sensible and necessary. Things can end in confrontation and stale-mate very quickly. Rules are often taken as personal criticisms, or just adults being bossy and controlling. The task is to try to help children view 'rules' differently. Rules are there to help us solve problems. For example: 'No running in the corridor'.

Most children will immediately recognise that this is intended to solve the problem of children getting hurt. 'No shouting out in class'. Most children will acknowledge that a classroom where everyone is shouting out would be an unpleasant place and a difficult one in which to learn. It is not too great a leap to begin a discussion of rules at home, for instance, rules around time spent on devices or limitations on the amount of sugar consumed.

In this cautionary tale we have a vehicle for presenting an alternative pattern. The story contains moments of humour likely to appeal to a young child, further lightening the mood and reducing resistance to seeing things from the adult's point of view. Young children in particular have a natural 'ego-centricity'. It is genuinely challenging for them to see the point of view of another person. In this story, the central protagonist has to first experience the consequences of their own behaviour before becoming able to drop their resistance and comply with the guidance which has been given. The child hearing the story, can absorb the pattern without having to experience the negative consequence for themselves.

1. **'The King's advisors':**

'The Bard': 'Peer pressure', 'personal values'.

'The Guardian': 'rules', 'limitations', 'laws'

'The Court Scientist': 'balancing rest and activity',

2. **'Royal Decree':**

'Rules aren't just grown-ups being bossy, they can be ways of solving problems'

3. 'Peace in the Kingdom':

This alternative view of rules can be useful for all children, but particularly for the child who may be on the ASD spectrum. If such a child can be assisted in identifying a persistent problem or difficulty and creating a rule for themselves relating to that issue, it can reduce the feeling of being 'out of control' or 'powerless' in the face of the problem. A sense of safety and autonomy is introduced which can often be of great help in reducing the problem or challenge faced. Where in the child's life do rules already help them to solve problems? Rules, then, can be characterised more broadly as strategies for problem solving. Children can produce their own lists of classroom rules, but with the emphasis always on which problem the rule solves. This positive perception of rules can be carried into academic learning. When a child understands that maths and literacy are also governed by rules and that strategies can be employed to make things easier, the sense of safety,

stability and empowerment experienced

can be a real aid to learning. When a child

is shown evidence of improvements in

their own performance with the

introduction of a few simple strategies, the

impact on confidence and learning can be

dramatic.

Yip, the smaller than average wolf

Once upon a time there was a family of

wolves. There was a mother wolf, a father

wolf, two strong brother wolves and two

strong sister wolves, and last of all, there

was Yip, a smaller than average wolf. They

called him Yip because that's the sound he

made when he

tried to howl like

the bigger wolves.

Yip's brothers and

sisters, and most

of the other young wolves in the pack

often made fun of him. At night, when the

moon came out, they would all gather

together and howl noisily into the night

sky, making a very impressive sound.

'Come on Yip', they would say, 'You're a

wolf, come and howl at the moon'. Keen to

join in, Yip would gather up all of his

strength and howl for all he was worth, but

all that came out was a tiny 'Yip'. The other

young wolves would roll about laughing.

This made Yip very sad and embarrassed.

All the wolves in the pack, especially the younger ones, would push Yip around, or simply not take any notice of him at all. They wouldn't let him join in their games and if he did try to join in, they would growl and snarl at him. This was very scary for Yip.

Time went by, as it does, and the other wolves continued to push little Yip around, ignore him, or make fun of him. One winter morning, Yip was minding his own business, having a snooze in a sheltered spot beneath the branches of a pine tree, by the river, when he heard a loud

commotion. Some of the older wolves had

returned from the hunt and they had

brought lots of juicy meat home with

them. This was exciting and important

because it was winter time and food was

scarce. The whole pack was very hungry

and there was angry competition for the

fresh meat.

Yip was very, very hungry. He hadn't eaten

for many days. He spotted a big, juicy

piece of meat which nobody else seemed

to have noticed and grabbed his

opportunity. As he turned to take his prize somewhere quiet to eat, an older, bigger wolf snatched it right out of his mouth. 'Give me that, Yip!' he snarled, giving Yip a real fright. But Yip really was hungry, so he tried again, finding a smaller piece of meat. He tried to sneak away quietly, without being noticed, but, 'Give me that, little Yip, I want it!'. Another big wolf snatched his dinner from him. Yip was shaking, but he was so hungry. He tip-toed nervously back to where the food was and picked up the tiniest scrap of meat, all that was left. He had only taken a few steps

when a huge, grey wolf leapt in front of

him and grabbed at the meat with his

huge, white teeth. Before he even had a

chance to think about it, Yip bared his

teeth and let out an enormous, terrifying

'GRRRRROOOOWWWLLLL'!!!

'Don't you dare touch my dinner', he

roared at the big, grey wolf, who turned on

his heels and scurried away with his tail

between his legs, very scared indeed.

Every single wolf in the pack turned to

stare at 'little' Yip, and it was only at that

moment that they realised he wasn't so

little anymore.

 They had

become so

used to

pushing him

around that they hadn't noticed him

growing into a fine, strong wolf. It was

only when they heard his powerful,

terrifying GRRRROOOOWWWLLL!!! That

they understood that they would have to

think very carefully indeed before they

tried to boss this wolf around. Yip was not

afraid any more. From then on, nobody ever called him 'little' Yip and if anyone was foolish enough to try to boss him around, all he had to do was use his great, big, terrifying, powerful

GGGRRRRROOOOOWWWWWLLLLLLLL!!!!!

Thinking about this story:

As an occasional meat-eater myself, I have, in recent months had to take a closer look at the impact and implications of meat-eating on the environment. While it would be inappropriate for me to try to influence thinking in either direction, I do believe it is an issue which has to be discussed. The story provides a springboard for that discussion.

Does being loud and aggressive make you more important? The social 'pecking order', whether it be in the classroom or with siblings and friends outside of school, can be hugely challenging, particularly for the more sensitive child. Such a child can, indeed, feel very small in those circumstances, and we have a duty to help them through it by providing positive, optimistic patterns for them to refer to.

1. 'The King's Advisors':

'The Bard':

Empathy, kindness, sharing.

Is it right for us to eat meat? Caring for our environment.

'The Guardian':

Bullies, abuse of hierarchies. Standing up for yourself. Getting the nourishment you need.

'The Court Scientist':

Growing up and changing. Measurement. How do we measure things? Is the same 'measuring stick' appropriate for different things? Should we measure, or judge all people by the same criteria?

2. 'Royal Decree':

'People who are quieter may have very important things to say'

'Everything changes over time, including people'

'Sometimes it is necessary to stand up to injustice. Even though it can be scary'

'It can be a mistake to make assumptions about people because sometimes they will surprise us'

'Sometimes we don't notice people, including ourselves, changing and growing up, but it is happening all the time'

3. **'Peace in the Kingdom':**

The sensitive child, the child who is physically smaller than their peers and especially the anxious child who perhaps feels psychologically smaller than their peers. Stop for a moment and consider just how difficult one day in school might be for such a child. The trials they face are now intensified by the pervasive influence of social media with its demands they look and 'be' a certain way. How do we help this child? The task is two-fold. Firstly, all children must be supported to develop empathy, kindness and generosity. The overwhelming majority of children will recognise the injustice inherent in the treatment of Yip and will exhibit protective, empathetic feelings towards him. Likewise, they will share in the discovery of his powerful voice. After

listening to the story. Children can be

encouraged, depending on their

developmental stage, to write, draw or talk

about both Yip and the other pack

members using adjectives or adjectival

phrases (e.g. 'scared', 'lonely', 'hungry',

'never gives up', 'brave', 'terrifying',

'intimidating', 'bullying', 'mean', 'selfish',

etc).

Most stories lend themselves to learning

about sequence and order as events in the

story unfold. This particular story is

deceptively sophisticated in this regard.

We are not told explicitly that enough time

has passed within the story for Yip to grow

into a formidable individual able to hold

his own in the pack. We are told only that

'time went by'. The child must perform the

cognitively challenging task of holding the

simple and immediate sequences of events

explicitly stated (eg the return from the

hunt and Yip's series of attempts to get

something to eat, culminating in success),

within the broader, implicit sequence of

events, (ie, Yip as a small, put-upon wolf-cub who, over time, grows into a wolf able to stand his ground and get his needs met).

On a more literal level, the story may inspire a wealth of activity around diet and getting the right balance of nourishment. As previously mentioned, this may include an exploration of ethical considerations around diet and environment.

Printed in Poland
by Amazon Fulfillment
Poland Sp. z o.o., Wrocław

57098401R10116